FOREST

FOREST

Published by Seoul Selection
105-2 Sagan-dong, Jongno-gu, Seoul, Korea
Phone: 82-2-734-9567, Fax: 82-2-734-9562
Email: publisher@seoulselection.com
www.seoulselection.com

Printed in the Republic of Korea

ⓒ 김흥숙, 2012.
1판2쇄 2015년 7월 17일

펴낸곳 서울셀렉션㈜
등록 2003년 1월 28일(제1-3169호)
주소 서울시 종로구 사간동 105-2 출판문화회관 지하 1층 (우110-190)
편집부 전화 02-734-9567 팩스 02-734-9562
영업부 전화 02-734-9565 팩스 02-734-9563
Email: publisher@seoulselection.com
www.seoulselection.com

ISBN: 978-89-97639-03-8 03810

FOREST 수 숲

Kim Heung-sook
김흥숙

Seoul Selection

Contents

집
Home

Contents

A Letter to All the Poets of the World

All people are born poets, but many of them are not aware of the fact. Only a few realize that they are poets, and then often only by chance. I think I am one of them.

While reading a book by the window, while strolling around neighborhood alleys, while parting with an old friend, or while putting up with something intolerable or struggling to understand something incomprehensible, I found words flowing out of me and committed them to paper. That is how the poems in this book were born.

Some poems come to life after a much longer, more complicated process of alchemy. Poets are as varied as people, and poems as varied as poets. As is written somewhere in this book, the Chinese character for poetry (詩) depicts a "temple of words."

Some temples are colorful and have charming wind chimes, whereas others don't even have wooden fish to their name. The poems in this book belong to the latter group. The temple here may be a simple ground without gates, walls, or even a house. It may have nothing more than a tree and a fountain, where anyone is free to enter or leave, sit or walk around.

Though they are short, I hope these poems will help people realize their true identity as poets. We are poets whether we write poems or not, whether our poems are published or not. This book, then, is a letter from one poet to all the poets of the world. I hope those who receive it will build as many of their own "temples of words" as possible, for writing poetry is one of the most beautiful ways of saving the world from becoming a darker place.

For their help in bringing these poems together from across my several notebooks, I wish to express my deep appreciation to Kim Hyung-geun, CEO-President of Seoul Selection, and his staff—the publishing coordinator, Eugene Kim; the designer, Lee Bok-hyun; and Colin Mouat, who compared the Korean and English versions. I would like to express special thanks to Ines Min, who did the final copy reading of the English version, and Yang Mi-soon, who inspired me to have these poems published.

Kim Heung-sook

세상의 모든 시인들에게 보내는 편지

사람은 누구나 시인으로 태어나지만 자신이 시인인 줄 모르고 살아가는 사람들이 많습니다. 아주 소수의 사람들만이 우연한 기회에 자신이 시인임을 알게 됩니다. 저도 그런 사람 중 하나일 겁니다.

창가에 앉아 책을 읽다가, 골목을 산책하다가, 오래된 벗과 헤어져 돌아오다가, 견디기 힘든 일을 견디다가, 이해할 수 없는 일을 이해하려 애쓰다가……, 그러다가 제 안에서 무엇인가 흘러 나왔고 저는 그것을 붙들어 종이 위에 앉혔습니다. 그렇게 저의 시들이 태어났습니다.

어떤 시들은 훨씬 어렵고 긴 연금의 과정을 거쳐 태어납니다. 시인의 종류는 사람의 종류만큼 많고 시의 종류는 시인의 종류만큼 많습니다. 이 책 어디선가도 얘기했지만 '시(詩)'는 그 한자가 뜻하는 것처럼 '언어의 절간'입니다. 절 중에는 단청과 풍경(風磬)이 화려한 절이 있는가 하면, 목어조차 없이 단출한 절도 있습니다.

이 시집의 시들은 아무래도 후자입니다. 문도 담도 없고 절집마저 없이, 나무 한 그루, 샘 하나만 있는 절터일지도 모릅니다. 누구나 들고 나며 앉았다 서성였다 할 수 있는 곳이지요.

이 짧은 시들이, 자신이 시인임을 잊고 사는 분들을 일깨웠으면 좋겠습니다. 시를 쓰거나 쓰지 않거나, 쓴 시를 책으로 묶어 출판하거나 하지 않거나, 우리는 모두 시인입니다. 이 책은 한 시인이 세상의 모든 시인들께 보내는 편지입니다. 이 편지를 받으신 분들이 가능한 한 많은 '언어의 절간'을 세우셨으면 좋겠습니다. 시를 쓰는 일은 세상의 악화를 막는 가장 아름다운 노력이니까요.

흩어져 있던 문장들을 한 권의 책으로 만들어 주신 서울셀렉션의 김형근 대표님과 편집자 김유진 씨, 디자이너 이복현 씨, 국문과 영문 원고를 대조해가며 보아주신 콜린 모우앳 씨, 영문 시 감수를 맡아주신 아이네스 민 씨, 그리고 이 시집을 낼 수 있게 영감을 주신 양미순 씨에게 마음으로부터 감사합니다.

2012년 5월 김홍숙

숲

Forest

봄 숲 I

3월은 가을의 이복자매
녹은 눈 젖은 낙엽
봄은 그 아래에서 온다
죽음 없이 태어나는 것
하나도 없다

Spring Forest I

March is autumn's half-sister.
Fallen leaves teary with melting snow.
Spring comes from underneath.
No birth without death.

봄 숲 Ⅱ

봄 숲은 의뭉스럽다
일주일 전에도 시치미 떼고 있더니
오늘은 어디로 보나 꽃이다

봄 숲은 잔인하다
일주일 전까진 알록달록 꽃뿐이더니
오늘은 오직 푸른 잎뿐이다

혹 숲에서 배웠을까
내 애인

Spring Forest II

Spring forest is secretive.
Until a week ago, it showed no sign,
yet flowers are everywhere today.

Spring forest is cruel.
Until a week ago, it was a rainbow garden.
Today, only green leaves.

Has he learned from the forest?
My love.

나무의 사랑

나무들이 서로를 어떻게
생각하는지 알고 싶으면
폭풍우 다음 날 숲으로 가라

재앙은
사랑을 증명하는 과격한 장치

The Love of Trees

If you want to know
how the trees care about each other, then
go to the forest the day after a storm.

Disasters
Extreme ways of proving love.

여름 숲 I

여름 숲에도 낙엽은 있다
대개는 덜 익은 빛깔 덜 여문 모양
완벽하게 물든 완전한 잎 드물다

요절한다고 다 천재는 아니다
요절한 사람 중에 천재가 있다

Summer Forest I

Summer forest has fallen leaves, too.
Most of unripe colors, of incomplete forms.
Rare are perfect leaves dyed spotless.

Not all those who die prematurely are geniuses;
geniuses are among those who die young.

여름 숲 II

바삭바삭 세상이 마르는 소리
귀가 막히면 저 소리를 못 듣겠지요
푸른 하늘에 흰 구름이 지천입니다
눈이 보이지 않으면 저 조화를 못 보겠지요

귀가 들리지 않아도 눈이 보이면
눈이 보이지 않아도 귀가 들리면
큰소리로 불평할 수 없습니다
귀가 들리고 눈까지 보이면
아무 것도 불평할 수 없습니다.

Summer Forest Ⅱ

Rustle, rustle, the world dries;
blocked ears cannot hear the sound.
Blue sky is strewn with white clouds;
blind eyes cannot see the sight.

If your ears are blocked but you are not blind,
if you are blind but your ears are not blocked,
you cannot complain loudly.
If your ears hear and your eyes see,
you cannot complain at all.

가을 숲 I

마른 잎 가을빛에도
향기는 푸르다
누우면 먼 곳으로부터
목관악기의 음성 흘러든다

아직 이승에 머물고 있는
친구들이 생각난다

Autumn Forest I

Dry leaves of autumnal colors
Yet a green fragrance;
I lie down and from afar
the voice of the woodwind flows in.

Friends who still remain on this earth
I come to think of.

가을 숲 Ⅱ

가을 숲 해는 더디게 오른다
꽃을 피우느라 애쓸 것 없으니
마침내 꽃이 된 잎들
그 마른 등을 비출 뿐

Autumn Forest II

The autumnal sun rises slow;
no need to rush to make flowers bloom.
Leaves become flowers at last;
just lighting their thin, dry backs.

은행나무 똥

하루 평균 1113그램의 똥을 싸고
2킬로그램에서 10킬로그램을 갖고 다니는 사람들이
은행나무 아래에서 얼굴을 찡그린다
은행이 벗어놓은 옷에서 똥 냄새난다고!

Ginkgo Shit

Producing an average of 1,113 grams of shit,
carrying between 2 and 10 kilos at any given time,
people make faces under ginkgo trees
crying that their seeds smell of shit!

겨울 숲 I

누구나 태어나 처음 본 얼굴을 사랑하니
눈은 백 살 먹은 나무를 사랑한다
사흘 낮 사흘 밤 순백 사랑 퍼부으니
'꿍!' 늙은 나무 제 한 팔 떼어준다

큰 나무의 가지들이 대칭을 이루지 못하는 건
사랑 때문이다

Winter Forest I

One loves the first face one sees;
so it is the hundred-year-old tree the snow loves.
For three days and three nights, white love pours;
groaning, the old tree gives one arm away.

Love leaves great tree branches asymmetrical.

겨울 숲 II

눈 없는 숲을
텅 빈 것이 채우고 있다

한때 연못은
이제 마른 잎 무덤

이윽고 고요하다

Winter Forest II

Snowless forest
packed with emptiness.

A pond once
Now a tomb of dry leaves.

Silence at last.

숲 I

커다란 손바닥
사람들은 손금 한두 개 골라 그리로만 간다
외로운 것들은 늘 몰려다닌다

거친 바람 후려친다
움직이지 말라고, 지금 여기 뿌리내리라고
외로움이 너를 키울 거라고

Forest I

A huge palm.
People choose only a couple of its lines;
the lonely move together always.

A gust of wind whacks;
don't move, take root where you stand,
for loneliness will help you grow.

숲 Ⅱ

숲을 들락거리는 건
바다를 항해하는 것과 같다
숲은 지나가는 자를 기억하지 않고
풍경은 여행자의 마음에만 남는다

Forest II

Going in and out of forest
is like sailing on the high seas.
Forest never remembers its travelers;
only in their hearts does the scenery last.

숲 Ⅲ

외로움을 이기지 못하는 사람들은
연못을 돌고
외로움을 이기려 하는 사람들은
나무들 사이로 들어간다

연못가엔 언제나 사람이 많다

Forest Ⅲ

Those who can't overcome loneliness
walk around the pond.
Those who want to overcome loneliness
walk among the trees.

Around the pond, there are always many people.

숲 Ⅳ

이슬의 목소리 듣고 싶으면
새벽 새의 지저귐 들으시라
햇살의 목소리 듣고 싶으면
시냇물의 속삭임 들으시라

소리 내는 것들은
소리 내지 못하는 것들을 위해 있으니

Forest IV

If you want to hear the voice of dewdrops,
listen to the chattering of early morning birds.
If you want to hear the voice of sunbeams,
listen to the whisper of splashing streams.

For those that make sounds
exist for those that cannot.

숲 V

저 까치가 식사를 마칠 때까지
기다려주어야 한다
저 딱따구리가 작업을 마칠 때까지
기다려주어야 한다
저 나무들이 우리가 떠날 때까지
기다려주듯이

Forest V

Have to wait until
the magpies finish eating.
Have to wait until
the woodpeckers finish working.
Just as the trees wait for us to leave.

숲 VI

나무를 베고 무를 심는 사람들을 보니
道가 게으름에서 나옴을 알겠다
나무 허리에 꽁꽁 묶어두고 싶다
배우라고!

Forest VI

Watching people cutting trees and planting radishes,
I realize awakening comes from idleness.
Wishing to bind them to the trees and say:
Learn!

숲 VII

입 큰 사람 둘이면
깊은 숲도 시장이다

귀 씻으러 숲에 왔다고?
나무들이 허리 꺾어 웃는다

Forest VII

When there are two big mouths,
deep forest is a market.

In the forest to clean out your ears?
Trees laugh, doubling over.

숲 Ⅷ

밤나무 자궁은
죽은 언니 아랫배

둥글게 부어오른 빗물 연못
이름 모를 벌레들 죽어라 배영 중

삶은 죽음에 깃든다

Forest VIII

Chestnut womb is
dead sister's underbelly.

In the rainwater pond swollen round
insects of no known name
backstroke desperately.

Life dwells in death.

산

산은 외로움을 먹고 자란다
오르고 내리는 발 저리 많아도
낮아지지 않는 건
사람들이 떨구고 오는 외로움 때문이다

Mountains

Mountains grow on loneliness.
So many feet mount and dismount,
yet mountains are not flattened
thanks to the loneliness people leave behind.

나무

이쪽 나무의 새들과
저쪽 나무의 새들이
얘기를 나눈다

새들의 말이 잠깐씩
내 머리 위에 앉았다 간다
나도 내가 나무인 줄 알았으니

Tree

Birds on this tree
Birds on that tree
Talk

For a short while their words
rest on my head and leave;
I thought I was a tree, too.

질경이

여린 질경이들
숲길 덮느라 바쁜데
잔등엔 벌써 무수한 발자국

태어나면서부터 밟히는 삶
사람의 세상이나 풀나무의 세상이나
다를 것 없다

Plantains

Young frail plantains
busy covering forest roads.
On their backs already
numerous footprints.

Lives trodden from their birth.
In the worlds of humans and plants,
no difference whatsoever.

애인

숲은 넓어도 새는 제자리에 앉는다

솔잎 위에 앉아 전화를 건다
새 소리 들었는가
솔 향내 맡았는가
용케도 숲인 걸 알아맞힌다
그러니 내 애인이다

My Love

The forest is wide, yet the birds sit where they sit.

Sitting on pine needles, I make a call.
Did he hear the bird sing?
Did he smell the pine?
How does he know I am in the forest?
So he is my love.

기다림

숲이 너무 아름답다고
애인에게 전화하면 안 된다
그가 가겠노라고 말하는 순간
당신의 기다림이 시작된다

나무들처럼 기다릴 수 없다면
아예 시작하지 않는 게 좋다

The Wait

The forest may be very beautiful,
but don't call your love to say so.
The moment he says he is coming
your wait will have begun.

Unless you can wait as the trees do,
you'd best not begin at all.

그리움

당신 보고 싶어 목마를 땐
막 오른 해 희미한 숲에 들어
덜 익은 햇살 두어 사발 들이킨다

그리움이란 것 별 것 아니다
여린 해에도 녹는 눈 같은 것이다

Longing

When thirsty from missing you,
I walk into the forest dim with just-risen sun
and drink two bowls of unripe sunlight.

Longing is trivial
like the snow melting under the frail sun.

처음으로

사십팔 년 이 개월 만에
호랑나비를 보았다

사십팔 년 삼 개월 만에
숲 속 낙엽 위에 누워보았다

늦게라도 보아야 하는 게 있다
늦게라도 해봐야 하는 게 있다

For the First Time

After forty-eight years and two months
I saw a swallowtail butterfly.

After forty-eight years and three months
I lay down on the autumn leaves in the forest.

There are things you need to see, however late.
There are things you need to do, however late.

길

Road

새의 충고

바늘 바늘 바늘비
날리나 그쳤나

전선 위의 작은 새 말없이
"입 닫아야 잘 보여!"

Advice from a Bird

Needle, needle, needle rain
Stopped or falling?

A silent little bird on the wire:
"The eyes see better when the mouth is shut!"

낙타 I

낙타가 사막을 건너는 이유
살기 힘든 소말리아에 사는 이유
나뭇가지 같은 사람들에게 젖 주는 이유
시속 65킬로미터로 달릴 수 있으면서
달아나지 않는 이유

얼굴 보고 알았다
우는 듯 웃는 듯한
그 사랑을 보았다

Camels I

Why camels cross the desert.
Why they live in stark Somalia.
Why they give milk to the twig-thin people.
Why they don't run away when they
can run up to 65 kilometers an hour.

Saw their faces and came to know.
Saw their love, half-smiling and half-crying.

낙타 II

왜 낙타만 사막을 건너느냐고?
그만한 낙관은 누구에게도 없으니!

Camels II

Why do only camels cross the desert?
No one else has that much optimism!

푸른 하늘

나흘 밤낮 울고
눈물 훔친 하늘
저리도 맑다
며칠 울고 나면
내 얼굴도 저와 같을까

Blue Sky

Tears wiped after four days
and four nights of sobbing.
Such a clean face the sky has.
How many days must I cry
before I have a face like that?

조금

길이 조금 젖어있어야
넘어지지 않는다

약간의 슬픔이
실수를 줄여주듯

A Little

When the road is a little damp,
you don't fall over.

When you are a little sad,
you make fewer mistakes.

교훈

은빛 날개는 얼굴로 날아들고
가뭇한 몸통은 손목의 점이 된다
오호, 나를 반기는가
미소로 답했는데
얼굴 간질 손목 따끔

반긴다고 다 친구는 아니다

Lesson

Silvery wings fly into the face,

black body becomes a mole on the wrist.

Oh, you welcome me!

I responded with a smile, but

face itches, wrist stings.

All that welcome you are not your friends.

눈

방향 없이 날리는 눈을 보며
저 눈처럼 사라진 사람들을 생각한다
이담에 저 눈 보며 내 생각할 사람들을 생각한다
저 눈처럼 차가워져야겠다

Snow

Looking at the snow floating in all directions
I think of those who vanished like the snow.
I think of those who might think of me someday
watching the snow.
I should be as cool as the snow.

눈물 어린 눈

눈의 눈이 반짝인다
먼 길 오느라 애썼다고
쓰다듬는 햇손 따스해
눈이 운다

Teary Snow

Eyes of snow shine:
"Such a long way you've come."
The sun's warm, caressing hands
make the snow cry.

2012년 1월의 눈

사람들이 일 년 만에
'복 많이 받으세요!'를 주고받자
하늘이 기뻐하며 하얀 복을 뿌려주었다
사람들이 미끄럽다며 염화칼슘을 뿌리자
시커먼 어제가 드러났다
또 다시 재앙 많은 한 해가 시작되었다

January 2012 Snow

For the first time in a year
people exchanged "Best wishes!"
Pleased, the heaven sprinkled its white blessing.
Fearful of slipping, people sprayed calcium chloride;
the dark yesterday surfaced.
Thus began another year of disasters.

삶

두 개의 문이 있는 찻집

반가운 사람 앞문에서 기다리다
뒷문으로 들어와 마중을 놓치고

뒷문으로 가려니 지키다가
앞문으로 사라져 배웅을 놓치는

Life

Waiting for the dear one at the front door
and missing the chance to welcome him;
he comes through the back door.

Waiting at the back door to see him off
and missing the chance to say goodbye;
he goes through the front door.

연애의 끝

여러 달 침묵하던 네게서
전화가 왔다
목소리 그대로이고
인사는 오히려 명랑한데

나는 아무렇지도 않다
젖은 재처럼 예의만 얌전하다

End of a Relationship

After months of silence
you called me up.
Voice the same as before,
greetings cheerful all the more.

I am not stirred;
just as proper as wet ashes.

봄

검은 눈 녹아 흐르는 길
영점 오 톤 꽃 트럭 한 귀퉁이
재스민 한 분
초록 손등에 흰 눈물 날리네

누군가 피어날 때
누군가는 죽어간다니까요

Spring

On the road, snow melts dark.
In the back of a half-ton flower truck,
a jasmine pot in the corner.
White tears falling on green hands.

When someone blooms,
someone dies, you know.

여행

길 위에선
새 사람을 만나고

길 아닌 곳에선
옛 사람을 만난다

Travel

On the road,
meeting the new.

Off the road,
meeting the old.

관광

뒤늦게 나선 벚꽃 구경
시드는 꽃 아래 마른 피 받침

남의 삶 사이 기웃거리며
제 상처를 만나는 것

Sightseeing

A belated viewing of cherry blossoms.
Bloody sepals drying under withering flowers.

Glancing through others' lives.
Coming across your own scars.

인사동

6시 반
석양은 낡은 얼굴들 위에 더 붉다

늙은이가 서두르지 않긴 어렵고
젊어지는 거리에 늙어가는 얼굴은 서먹해

게다가
젊은 얼굴에 어리는 제 옛 모습!

Insa-dong

Six thirty.
Sunset is redder on worn-out faces.

Hard not to hurry when you are old.
Aging faces uneasy on the rejuvenating street.

Even worse, your former self
looming on the young faces.

헤이리 연꽃

태어나는 순간부터 한 뜸 한 뜸
더는 자랄 수 없을 땐 발부리 돌려
저 깊디깊은 고향으로

다시 태어날 때까지

Heyri Lotus

From the moment of birth, inch by inch.
When growing is no longer possible,
turning the tips of toes around
towards the deep, deeper home

Until the moment of another birth.

모래에게 묻다

어제 종일 쏟아진 폭우는
어디로 갔을까
운동장의 모래들에게 묻는다
젖지도 않은

모래처럼 살아야겠다

Ask the Sands

Where has the downpour gone
after pounding all day yesterday?
Ask the sands in the playground;
they aren't even wet.

Should live like them.

황사

사하라, 파타고니아, 타클라마칸
한번쯤 시간의 몸을 보러가고 싶어도
달력에서 헤어나지 못하는 사람들
그들을 위해 사막이 온다
누런 바람 마차 타고

Yellow Dust

Sahara, Patagonia, Taklamakan.
Those longing to see the body of time,
yet confined in Gregorian calendars.
For them the deserts come
on the yellow windy wagon.

신에게 하는 충고

오늘 질경이 위에서 체조를 했다면
내일은 연못가에서
모레는 단풍나무 근처에서 해야 한다

신이 사람을 시험할 때도 그래야 한다
어제 맞은 사람 오늘 또 때리면 안 된다

매일 밟히면
질경이조차 일어서지 못한다

A Piece of Advice for God

If you exercise on plantains today,
you should do so by the pond tomorrow
and near the maple tree the day after.

God should do likewise when testing humans.
Shouldn't beat the one who got beaten yesterday.

If trodden every day,
even plantains cannot rise again.

신의 탄식

이렇게 맛있는 커피를 만들어주는 집에서
사람들은 소리 높여 돈 얘기만 한다

신도 탄식할지 모른다
이 향기 가득한 세상에서
고작 그렇게 살고 있냐고

God's Sigh

In this house of fine coffee,
people clamor only about money.

God may be lamenting, too:
In this world of fragrance,
how can you live only that way?

10월

금요일 첫차로 그대 도착하다
꼭 일 년 만에
그대도 반가운가, 흔들린다
때로 사랑은 말없이 함께 흔들리는 것

그믐밤 막차로 떠날 그대
벌써 그립다

October

On the first train Friday you came
after one full year.
You shake, perhaps happy too.
Love could mean shaking together, speechless.

On the last train on the last day
you will be leaving and I miss you already.

비

비 올 때 숲에 드는 자를 조심하라
젖는 것을 두려워하지 않으니

Rain

Beware those who enter the forest in the rain;
they are not afraid of getting wet.

재스민

재스민 꽃 핀 방은 거울 같아서
하품하기도 부끄럽지요
향기는 눈, 셀 수 없이 많은 눈이니까요

Jasmine

A room with jasmine flowers is like a mirror;
even yawning is an act of shame.
Fragrance is the eye, eyes too many to count.

이퀄라이저

늘 게으르던 심장이
하이트 두 병에 발랑발랑

말 없는 입으로 들어간 술은
말을 불러내고
말 많은 입으로 들어간 술은
말을 잠재운다

나이가 수십 년 걸려 하는 일을
술은 한 자리에서 해낸다

Equalizer

The lazy heart beats wild
after only two bottles of Hite.

Into a silent mouth
liquor goes to bring out words.
Into a talkative mouth
liquor goes to silence words.

What age does over several decades
liquor does in one sitting.

헤어짐

할 수만 있으면 골목어귀에서
헤어지지 말 일이다
골목은 작은 꽃
한 번 잡은 눈 놓아주지 않는다

할 수만 있으면 너른 길
사람들이 강으로 흐르는 곳에서
헤어질 일이다
아무리 용감한 연어도 역류할 수 없는 강

Parting

If possible, don't say goodbye
where the alley begins.
For an alley is a small flower;
eyes once caught won't be freed.

If possible, say goodbye
where people stream into a river,
where even the bravest salmon
can't swim back.

저 밤길 도둑고양이

우리가
그와 내가 된 순간, 그 후

시선 닿는 곳마다
저 네발 달린 침묵 혹은 곁눈질

The Stray Cat on the Night Road

That moment we became he and I
and from then on.

Wherever my eyes go,
the four-legged silence or sidelong glance.

저 달빛 불륜

붉은 등 아래
수컷 나무들이 길어 올린 씨물
골목을 적신다

스페르민, 구연산, 아미노산
아 아, 꽉꽉 채운 몸내
지나는 것들 모두 얼굴 붉히고
하늘엔 사내 없이 배부른 달!

The Moonlight Affair

Under the red lamps
semen drawn up by the male trees
wets the alleys.

Spermine, citrate, amino acids.
Ah, the fully packed smell of body.
All passers-by blush;
up in the sky the moon
pregnant without a male!

푸른 감

백일 후면 감다운 감일 텐데
젖은 길에 흩어진 초록 구슬들
그러게 생겨나지 말랬지
생겨났으면 죽어라 붙들고 있으랬지

Green Persimmons

Would have been real persimmons in a hundred days.
Green balls scattered on a watery road.
I told you never to be born,
and once born, cling on tooth and nail.

웃음 속의 벽

어떤 웃음 속에는
탁구대처럼 단단한 벽이 있다
내 마음이 그 벽에 부딪쳐서
튕겨 나온다

Walled Smile

Certain smiles have walls
as hard as the ping pong table.
My heart bumps against these walls
only to spring back.

피아노

곧게 뻗은 다리 위 활짝 열린 자궁
오르가즘으로 가는 여든 여덟 개의 열쇠
그런데
야상곡을 치고 나서 왜 땀을 흘리느냐고?

Piano

Wide-open womb over long straight legs.
Eighty-eight keys to orgasm.
So
why do I sweat after playing a nocturne?

빚쟁이들

씨 뿌리지 않는 자들은
씨 뿌리는 사람들에게
키우지 않는 자들은
자라는 것들에게
목사와 중과 신부는
믿는 사람들에게
정신노동자들은
육체노동자들에게
글 쓰는 자들은
살아가는 사람들에게

모두
빚지고 있다

The Debtors

Indebted are

those who don't sow seeds to all who do,
those who don't grow anything to all who do,
the pastor, monk, and priest to all who believe,
those who do mental labor to all who do physical labor,
those who write to all who live.

막다른 골목

세탁소 옆 골목은
빈 상자처럼 고요하다

길 하나 끝나는 곳에서
다른 길이 시작된다고 했지
성큼성큼 들어갔는데 막다른 길

모든 끝이 시작은 아니다

Blind Alley

The alley by the laundry
Quiet like an empty box

Where one road ends,
another begins, they say,
so I stride into it
only to find a dead end.

Not all endings are beginnings.

봉은사

절집 넓으나 눈 둘 곳이 없다
저 고층건물들 허리를 베어버리면?

엊그제 한밤중, 젊은 중들과 신도들의 불평을 견디지 못한
높은 스님이 아주 잘 드는 칼로 삼층까지만 두고 베어냈는
데, 잘라낸 것을 어디로 옮길까 둘러보아도 갖다 놓아 어울
릴 곳이 영 없어 다시 들고 왔다지, 소식을 들은 다른 높은
스님이 그래도 중들 눈 괴롭히는 게 낫지, 괴로움 없이 출세
간에 들 중이 어디 있는가, 죽비로 두어 번 먼지 털어 다시
제 자리에 놓았다지. 그래서 오늘 봉은사 머리 위가 그나마
맑다나.

Bongeunsa Temple

The precincts are wide yet the eyes cannot go far.
What if we cut the middle out of the high-rise buildings?

At midnight the other day, a senior monk who couldn't
stand the complaints of younger ones and worshippers
cut off the floors above the third with a very sharp sword
but wondered where to put those floors, finally bringing
them back when he couldn't find anywhere they would
fit; another elder heard the story and, saying it'd be better
to torment monks' eyes, for no seeker would attain
awakening without troubles, dusted off the cut-offs with a
split bamboo rod and put them back in place. That's why
the sky over Bongeunsa Temple is a little clearer today.

밤

밤엔
눈 뜬 자들만 돌아다닌다
어둠으로
낮에 본 것들을 지우려함이다

눈먼 자는 밤길을 걷지 않는다
지울 것 없으니

Night

Roaming about at night
are wide open eyes only
trying to erase with darkness
what was seen during the day.

The blind don't walk around at night;
they have nothing to erase.

그들은 모른다

이른 아침 눈 덮인 대지의 등을 긁는
사람들은 모른다
곳곳의 부스럼 보다 못한 하늘이
부드럽고 흰 거즈 덮어주었다는 것

때론 무언가를 하지 않는 것이
하는 것보다 정의롭다는 것

They Know Not

Those who scrape the back of the snow-covered earth
from early in the morning know not
that the merciful heavens couldn't bear the sores
all over and draped soft white gauze on her.

That sometimes not doing is closer to justice than doing.

엄마 냄새

엄마 앉았던 곳에 파스 냄새
엄마 누웠던 곳에도 파스 냄새
엄마 어깨에 파스를 붙이며
으음, 엄마 냄새!

나 없어지고 나면
약국 가서 날 찾겠네
하 하 웃는다, 우리 엄마

오래된 농담이 슬픔을 일으키는 날
그런 날은 영영 오지 않았으면

Mom's Smell

The smell of menthol patches
where mom sat or lay.
Plastering her shoulder:
Mm, the smell of mom!

After I am gone,
will you look for me at the drugstore?
My mom laughs, Ha ha.

When an old joke stirs sorrow.
Wish such a day would never come.

백련사

산비둘기 소리 들으려
절 마루에 앉았더니
문 닫힌 방마다 목탁새 운다

Baengnyeonsa Temple

Sat on the temple floor
to hear the mountain dove;
From every closed door
cry wooden gong birds.

고열

무례한 손님
전화도 없이 찾아왔다
인사도 없이 떠나가는

혹은
말없는 스승
너무 열심히 뛰지 말라고
그 길이 그 길인지 잠시 생각하라고

High Fever

Impolite guest
coming without calling,
going without a goodbye.

Or
Silent teacher:
Don't run too fast.
Think for a bit
whether you are on the right road.

별

바람은 굶주린 짐승
강아지도 고양이도
어디로 들어가 숨고
우왕좌왕 갈 곳 모르는 낙엽

꿈쩍 않는 것은 별들뿐

높아지라고
단단해지라고
반짝이라고

지나가는 것들에
겁먹지 말라고

Stars

Wind is a hungry beast;
puppies and kittens go into hiding.
Autumn leaves run about not knowing where to go.

Unwavering are stars only.

Go higher.
Be sturdier.
Do twinkle.
Don't ever be afraid of passing things.

아기와 노인

갓 태어난 얼굴은 모두 닮아 있다
곧 죽을 얼굴도 모두 닮아 있다
출발선의 얼굴은 모두 닮아 있다

Babies and Seniors

Newborn faces are all alike.
Moribund faces are all alike.
Faces at the starting line are all alike.

가끔

가끔 생각합니다
마음에 있으면
만나지 않아도
상관없다고

또 가끔 생각합니다
마음에 있어도
한 번은 보아야 한다고

From Time to Time

Sometimes I think
it doesn't matter if I see you or not
as long as you are on my mind.

Other times I think
I have to see you at least once,
even if you are on my mind always.

집
Home

나이 I

이백 예순 여섯 살 소나무 아래
작은 나무들과 질경이를 보며
십팔 세기를 생각한다

작은 나무들이 이백 예순 살쯤 되고
질경이가 햇빛 찾아 긴 터널을 지나가는
이십삼 세기 어느 날, 누군가는 오늘 나처럼 서성이리라

Age I

Under a two hundred sixty-six-year old pine tree,
seeing shrubs and plantains,
I think of the eighteenth century.

One day in the twenty-third century
when the shrubs will be two hundred and sixty-something
and plantains pass through a long tunnel to find sunlight,
someone might wander about as I'm doing today.

나이 II

서른이 되어서는 천재가 아니라는 걸 알았고
마흔이 되어서는 생활인도 못 된다는 걸 알았다
쉰이 되면 무엇을 알게 될까
예순이 되고 일흔이 되면 또 무엇 무서운 것을?
모든 것을 알려면 얼마나 오래 살아야 할까
혹은 얼마나 여러 번?

Age II

When I was thirty, I knew I wasn't a genius.
At forty, I knew I wouldn't even be ordinary.
At fifty, what will I learn?
At sixty, at seventy, what dreadful things?
How long must one live to understand everything?
Or how many times?

나이 III

나이 먹는 건 산에 오르는 것
오르면 오를수록 잘 보인다
보려고 한다면

Age III

Aging is mountain climbing.

The higher you climb, the better you see.

Only if you want to see.

노화의 제 문제

노화의 문제는 대개
몸은 늙는데 마음은 늙지 않아 생긴다

마음이 앞서 늙어
언젠가 늙은 몸이 도달할 그곳에
먼저 가서 기다리면
아무런 문제도 생기지 않을 텐데

The Many Problems of Aging

Aging causes problems
because the body ages
while the mind doesn't.

If the mind aged fast,
reached and waited where
the aged body would arrive,
there would be no problem.

새해 I

눈보라 숲에서 돌아오는 길
숲으로 가는 발자국 보았네
나 말고도 숲으로 간 사람 있구나
반가워 그 옆에 내 발자국 찍어보니
이런, 바로 내 발이었네!

외로운 길에서 나를 만났네
새해엔 더 많이 외로워져야겠네

New Year I

Returning from the forest in a snow storm,
I saw somebody's footprints headed back.
So I wasn't the only one to go into the forest!
Gladly put my feet beside the prints.
What do you know?
They were no one else's but mine!

Came across myself on a lonely road.
Should be lonelier in the New Year.

새해 II

해가 바뀔 때마다
주소록이 얇아진다

소리 없는 이름들 보듬고 있다가
마침내 헌 잎 떨구는 나무가 된다

New Year II

Year after year,
thinner becomes my address book.

Keep the voiceless names for some time,
then become a tree shedding old leaves.

의문

시인의 부음을 읽으며
애인이 사다준 피칸파이를 먹는다
입 안에 퍼지는 피칸 향내
피칸은 살아있는가, 죽은 건가?
나는?

Question

Reading a poet's obituary,
I eat a pecan pie my sweetheart bought me.
Mouth-filling pecan aroma.
Is the pecan alive or dead?
How about me?

시 I

시계가 열두 번을 친다
발은 산을 그리워해도
손은 노트 위에 머문다
어둔 산의 살비듬이 조금씩
노트 위에 쌓여간다

Poetry I

The clock strikes twelve times.
The feet long for the mountain;
the hand lingers on the notebook.
Little by little, flakes of dark mountain
pile on the notebook.

시 II

누군가 보고 있을 땐
손바닥에라도 끼적이지 말 일이다
"시인이세요?" 하고 물을 수 있으니까

수업시간에 사탕을 먹듯 물고 있다가
아무도 보지 않는 곳에 가서 떨궈야한다
어미새가 아기새 입에 벌레를 떨구듯

Poetry II

When somebody's watching,
don't even scribble on your palm;
he might ask, "Are you a poet?"

Hold it like a candy you eat in class.
Unload it somewhere when nobody's watching
like a bird dropping insects into a chick's mouth.

문학에게 목표가 있다면

잠든 영혼을 깨우는 것
잠든 자의 영혼까지도

정복당하기를 거부하는 것
심장 없는 자 앞에서도

미워하지 못하는 것
미움 받기 위해 태어난 자까지

If Literature Has a Goal

Waking up sleepy spirits,
even the spirits of the sleeping.

Refusing to be conquered,
even by the heartless.

Being unable to hate
even those born to be hated.

생후 56년 9시간 현재 그녀의 가방 속

먹다 남은 바게트 두 조각, 요구르트 한 개, 노트 두 권, 햇빛 아래서 양산이 되는 초록 우산, 검은 뚜껑이 달린 분첩, 새빨간 연지, 볼펜 세 자루, 몇 개의 이름들과 전화번호와 주소가 적힌 초콜릿 색 표지의 수첩, 검은색 가죽 지갑, 만 원짜리 세 장, 신용카드 세 개, 시립도서관 출입증, 버스카드, 바늘쌈지, 여행용 클리넥스, 휴대전화, 바랜 빨간 손수건.

즉, 언제라도 버릴 수 있는 모든 것

In Her Purse as of Fifty-Six Years and Nine Hours After Birth

Two leftover pieces of baguette, a bottle of yogurt, a couple of notebooks, the green umbrella that becomes a parasol under the sun, a powder compact with a black lid, a flaming red lipstick, three ballpoint pens, a chocolate-colored memo pad with a few names and phone numbers and addresses, a black leather billfold with three 10,000-won bills, three credit cards, a pass for the public library, a bus card, a needle pad, a traveler's Kleenex, a cellular phone, a faded red handkerchief.

A whole bunch of dispensable things.

나는 누구인가

나의 냉정함은 때로 나를 놀라게 한다
하루 동안에 여덟 명의 걸인을 외면했다
나의 잔인함은 때로 나를 놀라게 한다
하루 동안에 네 마리의 벌레를 죽였다

세 끼의 밥과 세 잔의 커피를 먹고
자정도 되지 않아 누워 눈을 뜨니 아침
나는 때로 내가 무섭다

Who Am I?

My coldness surprises me sometimes;
in one day, I have turned away eight beggars.
My cruelty surprises me sometimes;
in one day, I have killed four bugs.

Had three meals and three cups of coffee,
lay down before midnight, woke up to find morning.
I scare the shit out of me sometimes.

새벽

소위 새로 1시 25분

어디서는 쓰레기들이 차에 오르고
누구에게선 다섯 개의 줄이 뽑히고
산동네 마른 골목마다 아카시아 몸내가 흥건한

누군가는 레테 강을 건너고
누군가의 품속으론 고양이 같은 애인이 파고들고
누군가의 노트엔 절간* 하나 일어나는

---

*시는 '詩'이다. 즉 '언어(言) 로 지은 절(寺)'이다.

Dawn

The so-called first hour and twenty-fifth minute.

Somewhere garbage mounts a truck.
Somebody has five tubes taken out.
Every skinny alley of the hillside slum
brims with the bodily smell of acacia.

Somebody crosses the River Lethe.
Into somebody's arms crawls a cat-like lover.
On somebody's notebook a temple* rises.

_____

*The Chinese character for "poetry" is 詩, meaning "a temple of words."

컴퓨터 선승

흰 화면에 주절주절 썼던 것 다 지우고
ⓧ 눌러 창 없는 창 닫으려 하니
녀석이 묻는다, '저장할까요?'

야, 이 바보야, 아무 것도 없는데 무얼 저장해?
녀석이 태연히 답한다, '당신이 남기신 텅 빈 충만.'

Computer Zen Monk

After writing, then deleting everything on the white surface,
I click ⓧ to close the windowless window;
and it asks, "Will you save it?"

You moron. Nothing's there, what can I save?
It answers nonchalantly:
"The empty fullness you've left."

불면

잠도 추억도 잘못된 시간에만 찾아온다

일당에 지친 몸이 녹슨 샤워꼭지 아래
문명인을 도모할 때
물 한 줄기에 한 움큼씩 자라나는 속눈썹
간신히 다가간 침상엔
눈 부릅뜬 어제들이 마스터베이션 중

Insomnia

Sleep and memories always come at the wrong hours.

When the wage-beaten body tries
to civilize itself under the rusty tap,
eyelashes grow a span with each stream of water.
Stumbling to the bed;
wide-eyed yesterdays masturbating.

Credits

Author	Kim Heung-sook
Publisher	Kim Hyung-geun
Editor	Kim Eugene
Copyeditor	Colin Mouat, Ines Min
Designer	Lee Bok-hyun

글쓴이	김흥숙
펴낸이	김형근
편 집	김유진
영문 감수	Colin Mouat, Ines Min
디자인	이복현